Dear mou[...]
Welcome to the world of

Geronimo Stilton

The Editorial Staff of
The Rodent's Gazette

1. Linda Thinslice
2. Sweetie Cheesetriangle
3. Ratella Redfur
4. Soya Mousehao
5. Cheesita de la Pampa
6. Mouseanna Mousetti
7. Yale Youngmouse
8. Toni Tinypaw
9. Tina Spicytail
10. William Shortpaws
11. Valerie Vole
12. Trap Stilton
13. Branwen Musclemouse
14. Zeppola Zap
15. Merenguita Gingermouse
16. Ratsy O'Shea
17. Rodentrick Roundrat
18. Teddy von Muffler
19. Thea Stilton
20. Erronea Misprint
21. Pinky Pick
22. Ya-ya O'Cheddar
23. Mousella MacMouser
24. Kreamy O'Cheddar
25. Blasco Tabasco
26. Toffie Sugarsweet
27. Tylerat Truemouse
28. Larry Keys
29. Michael Mouse
30. Geronimo Stilton
31. Benjamin Stilton
32. Briette Finerat
33. Raclette Finerat

Geronimo Stilton
A learned and brainy
mouse; editor of
The Rodent's Gazette

Thea Stilton
Geronimo's sister and
special correspondent at
The Rodent's Gazette

Trap Stilton
An awful joker;
Geronimo's cousin and
owner of the store
Cheap Junk for Less

Benjamin Stilton
A sweet and loving
nine-year-old mouse;
Geronimo's favorite
nephew

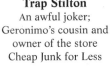

Geronimo Stilton

THE PHANTOM OF THE SUBWAY

Scholastic Inc.

New York   Toronto   London   Auckland   Sydney
Mexico City   New Delhi   Hong Kong   Buenos Aires

No part of this publication may be reproduced, stored in a retrieval system, or transmitted in any form or by any means, electronic, mechanical, photocopying, recording, or otherwise, without written permission from the copyright holder. For information regarding permission, please contact: Atlantyca S.p.A., Via Leopardi 8, 20123 Milan, Italy; e-mail foreignrights@atlantyca.it, www.atlantyca.com.

ISBN 978-0-439-66162-1

Published by Scholastic Inc., 557 Broadway, New York, NY 10012. SCHOLASTIC and associated logos are trademarks and/or registered trademarks of Scholastic Inc.

Stilton is the name of a famous English cheese. It is a registered trademark of the Stilton Cheese Makers' Association. For more information, go to www.stiltoncheese.com.

Text by Geronimo Stilton
Original title *Il fantasma del metrò*
Cover by Larry Keys
Illustrations by Blasco Tabasco and Guy Codana; revised by Federatto Brusco
Graphics by Merenguita Gingermouse and Topea Sha Sha

Special thanks to Kathryn Cristaldi
Translated by Joan L. Giurdanella
Interior design by Kay Petronio

40 39 38 37 36 35 34 33 32 31   14 15 16/0

Printed in the U.S.A.   40
First printing, November 2004

TERROR IN THE SUBWAY

Cheese niblets! The subway was chasing me! My heart was racing. My teeth were chattering. My ears were ringing.

I woke up with a start. Pheew, it was only a dream! That's right. I was safe and sound in my bed. My ears weren't *RINGING*. But the phone was. I picked it up. "Hello, *Geronimo Stilton* squeaking."

My sister's shriek made

me jump. "Geronimooo! Get your tail to the office. **Right NOW!** It's important!" Thea yelled.

I looked at the clock and leaped.

Whaaat? Ten minutes past nine? I was terribly *late*!

"I'm on my way," I told my sister. But I was talking to a dial tone. One thing you should know about my sister. She's not the most patient mouse on the block.

I JUMPED in the shower, brushed my teeth, and got dressed in record time.

Then I rushed to the Singing Stone Plaza subway station.

I was waiting for my train when I heard

a **horrifying** sound.

MEOOOOOOWWW!!!

The crowd rushed for the stairs, squeaking in terror. "A CAT! There's a CAT in the subway!"

I ran for the exit, too. It was bad enough I was late for work. I wasn't about to become some cat's breakfast sandwich! Rodents

SINGING STONE PLAZA

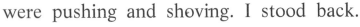

were pushing and shoving. I stood back. Oh, yes, I wanted to save my tail. But I didn't want to be crushed to a **FURRY PULP**. Just then, I noticed an elderly lady holding a young mouse by the paw. "Come on, Grandma," the little mouse cried. But the old lady mouse was frozen with *fear*.

Quickly, I grabbed her paw. "Don't worry, madam," I yelled. "Everything is going to be all right." I scooped up the young mouse. Then I led them both up the stairs.

At last, we were outside.

"Thank you, you are a true *gentlemouse*!" squeaked the old lady gratefully.

I smiled. Do you like to help others? I do. It makes me feel all warm inside. Sort of like when you eat a delicious bowl of hot cheddar soup.

Thinking of soup reminded me that I had forgotten to eat breakfast. I was starving. I bought the little mouse a cheese ICE CREAM. Then I had one, too. Not my typical breakfast. But then this was not a typical morning.

A PHANTOM CAT

I looked at my watch. It was ten o'clock already! I had to get to the office right away.

Oops, I almost forgot. I never introduced myself. My name is Stilton, *Geronimo Stilton*. I run *The Rodent's Gazette*. It is the most popular newspaper here on Mouse Island.

Thea is the paper's special correspondent.

Now, let's see, where was I? Oh yes, I was on my way to the office. I decided to hail a taxi. When I arrived at the *Gazette*, I looked for my sister.

Suddenly I heard the roar of a motorcycle. The door flew open and there she was.

I groaned. "Thea, how many times do I have to tell you?" I squeaked. "Don't ride your bike into my office!"

She just giggled. Then she parked her bike next to my desk. "Forget the bike, Gerry Berry," she ordered. "I've got bigger news. It seems there's a humongous cat in the subway. It may even be a ghost! We **ab-so-lute-ly** have to beat *The Daily Rat* to the scoop!"

I tried to tell Thea about the meowing in the subway. But she wasn't listening. Once my sister gets on a roll, there is no stopping her. She's like the *Apollo Swiss Cheese* rocketing into space. Three . . . two . . . one . . . blast off!

Now she raced to the COMPUTER and started surfing the Net.

"Here it is!" she shrieked, making me jump. You should know another thing about my sister. She is VERY excitable. She began to read the latest news on the mysterious cat. It went something like this:

On Monday, rodents reported smelling CAT pee-pee at the Cheese Rind Subway station.

On Tuesday, someone found strange CATlike scratches at the Scurryhill station.

On Wednesday, huge CAT prints were

found at the Nibble Drive station.

On Thursday, horrified passengers spotted a **CAT**'s shadow at the Curlyfur Court station.

On Friday (that's today), an awful **CAT**'s meowing was heard at the Singing Stone Plaza station. Rumor had it that the **CAT** was a ghost. Yes, an honest-to-goodmouse, horrible, horrifying, hideous ghost **CAT**!

I chewed my whiskers. "Can you please stop using that word?" I begged Thea. "You know I am terribly afraid of **CATS**."

My sister snorted. "Geronimoid," she smirked. "You are afraid of everything. In fact, if you weren't a mouse, I'd call you a 'fraidy **CAT**!"

I felt faint with fear. My sister has no sympathy for a mouse of my delicate nature.

ANYONE FOR GOLF?

At that moment, I noticed a fax coming in. It was a press bulletin.

"Inspector Clue Rat closes the subway for safety reasons!" it screamed.

Thea twirled her tail. "I just have to know more!" she cried. She picked up the phone and began calling all of her big-shot friends: the mayor of New Mouse City; the chief of police; the city's top cheese inspector; the world's most famouse detective, Hercule Poirat. . . .

She put down the receiver, looking disappointed.

"Rats! This is just **un-be-liev-a-ble!** No one

Hercule Poirat

will tell me anything about the subway case!" she complained.

By now, it was already late afternoon.

Suddenly, an idea hit me. "Did I tell you that I've taken up golf again?" I said.

My sister put her paws on her hips. "Geronimo, I'm talking about a huge scoop," she grumbled, "and you're talking about golf. You are so foolish! You are so thick! You are such a *cheesehead*!"

I rolled my eyes. Why did my sister love to pick on me? I was a good mouse. I never hurt anyone. Well, there was that one time when I accidentally ran over Uncle Nibbles's tail

Birdie
Whiskers

with my car. But that's another story. . . .

"For your information, Thea," I said, "I happen to have just met Birdie Whiskers down at the golf club."

My sister raised her eyebrows. I could tell she was impressed. That's because Birdie Whiskers was always in the news. He was a *championship golfer*. And besides winning tournaments, he also was the head of the entire subway system.

I picked up the phone and called Birdie. I congratulated him on his latest game. Then I asked him about the mystery in the subway. Unfortunately, not even Birdie could talk to me. The investigation was *top-secret*.

I hung up with a deep sigh.

Suddenly, my cousin Trap barreled through the door. Of course, he didn't bother to knock. I don't think he even knows how. Yes, that cousin of mine is one pushy mouse. In fact, his nickname is Pushy Paws.

I stared at him now. He was loaded down with shopping bags.

"Have you heard the news? I am going to open my own bagel place!" he shrieked. "I'm going to call it **BIG BELLY BAGELS** FOR BIG-BELLIED RODENTS."

WHAT'S UP, COUSINKINS?

Trap dumped his bags on my floor. Then he pulled the wrapper off a cheddar lollipop. "What's up, Cousinkins?" he asked, plopping into my chair. He put his paws up on my desk. Then he started picking his snout.

"Do you mind?" I squeaked.

I shook my head in despair. Did I mention Trap can be a complete **slob** sometimes? It's a wonder we are related!

He pulled the LOLLIPOP out of his mouth and burped. "Well, somebody forgot

"What's up, Cousinkins?"

to take their anti-grouchy pill this morning," he smirked.

He stuck his sticky lollipop in his pocket. Then he began cleaning his teeth with a toothpick.

By this time, I had had enough. I slammed my paw on my desk.

"Trap, can't you see we are busy?" I burst out. "We are working on a story about the PHANTOM in the subway. It's **big** news!"

His eyes grew wide. "Big news, huh?" he muttered, deep in thought. Then he grinned. "Don't worry, Germeister. I can handle this one," he said. "Just sit back and watch a pro at work."

Before I could squeak, he grabbed the phone and started dialing. "I've got friends in all the right places, you see," he explained. "Simpleton Smallpaw is the

nephew of the doormouse for the building where the head of the entire New Mouse City Transit Authority lives. Yep, Simp and I play checkers together every week at the ***Telltail Tavern***."

Seconds later, he was chatting away on the phone. First he told some awful jokes. Then he made some rude noises. Finally, he got down to business. "Listen, Simp, I'd love to blab all day, but I've got work to do. I need some info about that **CAT** in the subway," he said.

Ten minutes later, he hung up. A big smile spread across his face.

"I know everything!" he squeaked. "Am I **GOOD** or what?"

I tried not to roll my eyes. After all, I wanted to hear Trap's information. Still, it wasn't easy. I wanted to knock his paws off

Trap grabbed the phone.

my desk. I wanted to throw his sticky lollipop out the window. But more than any of that, I wanted the s c o o p.

I leaned forward. "Well?" I asked in my nicest voice. "What's the news?" Beside me, Thea grabbed her notebook, pencil in paw.

But instead of spilling the beans, my cousin just snickered. He twirled his tail, looking smug. *Uh-oh,* I thought. When Trap gets that look, it can mean only one thing. Trouble with a capital **T**!

SECRET
INFORMATION

I was right. Trap wasn't about to give his news away for free. He wanted to be paid. "I could use a few smackeroos," he said. "I mean, I am opening up *BIG BELLY BAGELS*, you know."

I should have known. Trap is always looking for money. And **I** am his favorite mousey bank.

"Here is my offer," my cousin went on. "I will give you the inside scoop on the **CAT** in the subway. You will publish a special edition of the paper. Of course, it will make lots and lots of money. Then we will divide up the dough: **80** percent for me, **20** percent for you."

"What?! Are you crazy?" I squeaked. I

was fuming. What did I do to deserve such an obnoxious relative? He was so frustrating. He was so **ANNOYING**. He was enough to drive a mouse up a clock!

My cousin pretended to be shocked. "Listen, Gerry Berry," he squeaked. "You're lucky I'm giving you any info at all. In fact, maybe I should just make a deal with Sally Ratmousen. I bet she'd hand over some **cash** to get the scoop on this **CAT**."

I turned pale. Do you want to know why? Sally Ratmousen is my archrival. She is the owner of *The Daily Rat,* my paper's biggest competition!

YOU ARE SUCH A PENNY-PINCHER, GERONIMO

I jumped to my paws. "That's ridiculous!" I screeched. "You know Sally is my number-one enemy!"

Trap just sighed. "It's your own fault, Geronimoid," he insisted. "If you weren't such a penny-pincher, you'd have your story."

PENNY-PINCHER?! I couldn't believe my ears. I am a lot of things: a scaredy mouse, a brainiac, a worrywart. But I am not a penny-pincher. Every year, I give dozens of free books to the Rattown Library. And on Christmas, I send a hundred cheddar logs to the residents at the Creaky Mouse Nursing Home. Why, I would give my right paw for a rodent in need! I was so MAD, I couldn't squeak.

But it didn't matter. My sister had started screaming at Trap. Her ear-piercing squeak made my head pound. I was getting a mouse-sized headache.

Right then, Pinky Pick* marched into the room. One look at Pinky's face and

I realized that she had heard everything.

*Pinky Pick is my very young assistant editor. She is just fourteen years old. She goes to school in the morning, then works for the *Gazette* in the afternoon.

IT'S A DEAL!

Pinky PICK

Pinky hopped up and down on her pink platform shoes. "Everyone freeze!" she ordered.

Thea stopped yelling at Trap. Trap stopped yelling at Thea. I stopped chewing my whiskers. All eyes turned to my assistant editor.

Pinky is only a teenager, but she is not shy. In fact, she is the exact OPPOSITE. When that mouse starts squeaking, look out. She can talk the fur off a long-haired hamster!

"OK, here's the deal," she began.

It's a deal!

1. *Trap tells us everything he knows.*
2. *I tell you how to get by the police barricades in the subway.*
3. *Thea organizes the whole expedition.*
4. *And, Boss, you put up the dough.*

She grinned and went on. "We'll divide the money among all four of us. That's **25** percent for everyone," she finished.

Trap groaned. "What? Equal shares?" he complained. "That doesn't sound fair."

Pinky twirled her tail. "Take it or leave it," she squeaked cheerfully.

For a moment, no one said a word. It was so quiet, you could have heard a sliver of Parmesan drop.

Then Trap stuck out his paw. "It's a deal!" he told Pinky. They shook paws.

I could tell Trap wanted more money. But I could also tell something else. He was impressed with my tough-talking assistant. Who would guess a little mouse in pink shoes could be so pushy?

A FIVE-HUNDRED-
POUND FELINE?

We got right down to work. Trap listed all of the new info he had received from Simpleton Smallpaw.

1. New **CAT** scratches had been found on the cheese-pop vending machine at Scurryhill station.

2. Crimerat experts had examined the scratches. They concluded the cuts had been made by a twenty-foot-tall **CAT** who weighed more than five hundred pounds!

3. At Cheese Rind station, they found tufts of fur and a ten-foot-long **CAT** whisker.

4. The catology expert from the Mouseum of Rodent History said the mysterious **DARK GRAY** feline could be a gigantic specimen of *Colossal catitus.*

5. A feline psychology professor was working on a top-secret trap for the subway **CAT**. It involved a gigantic cage and four hundred boxes of Kitty Krunchies.

FOUR SUPER-SPICY PIZZAS!

When Trap finished, Thea grabbed the phone. She dialed the number for Rats Authority, the best store in town for sporting goods. "Yes, I'll need four wet suits, four pairs of **rubber** boots, four flashlights . . ." she ordered. The list went on and on. I sighed. I had a feeling this expedition was going to cost me more than a five-course meal at Le Squeakery, my favorite French restaurant.

Trap used the phone next. He called the pizza place across from my office. "Hello? Send me four super-spicy, super-cheesy, super-large, super-expensive pizzas with **everything** on them. Right away!"

I groaned. Did he have to add expensive?
Even pizza can get pricey in a place like
New Mouse City.

He was about to hang up when he shouted
one last order. "One more thing," he added.
"Make my cousin's pizza extra **SUPER-
SPICY**. He needs to strengthen his stomach!"

I started to protest.
Eating spicy food
could kill me. I'm
not kidding.
One time, I
accidentally
ate a burrito
at Hotfur's
Mexican Cantina.
My stomach was
messed up for **months**!

super-spicy, super-cheesy, super-large, super-expensive pizzas with everything on them

I was still thinking about Hotfur's when

Thea grabbed my paw. "You're coming with us, Geronimo, aren't you?" she asked.

I didn't say a word. There was no way I was going down into the subway's dark, SPOOKY tunnels. Plus, I didn't want to come snout-to-snout with a gigantic CAT!

"Ahem, well, actually, I feel like I might be getting a cold," I explained.

Just then, Trap piped up. "My good friend Whiskers Malone told me that Sally Ratmousen is following the same hot trail. You wouldn't want her to beat us to the scoop, would you?" he announced.

Rats! Just hearing Sally's name made my tail twitch. As terrified as I was about encountering the phantom CAT, I knew I had to do it. I couldn't let that rotten Sally Ratmousen beat me at my own game.

The Rodent's Gazette had to get the story before *The Daily Rat* did!

"I'm in!" I declared. I just hoped I wasn't *in* for trouble.

EAT, DRINK, AND BE SQUEAKY!

Moments later, the doorbell rang. It was the pizza delivery.

Trap ate his pizza in one **gulp**. He ate half of mine, too. Just looking at it gave me **HEARTBURN**.

Thea put film in her camera and stuffed it into her backpack.

Trap stuffed his pack with food. "**Eat, drink, and be squeaky!**" he chuckled.

The doorbell rang again.

This time it was the delivery from Rats Authority.

With a sigh, I put on my wet suit and rubber boots. I pulled on a helmet with a

flashlight attached to the brim. Across one shoulder I had a sturdy rope with a hook on the end. I PRAYED NO ONE WOULD SEE ME. I LOOKED RIDICULOUS. I mean, I don't have the body for adventure gear. Plus, I am a professional mouse. I like my suits and ties.

At last, we were ready. Ready for anything. At eight o'clock, we left. It was almost dark outside. We looked more like burglars than journalists hunting for a scoop.

Pinky took us to a NARROW alley at the back of the fish market.

She showed us a drain. "All the subway entrances have been closed by the police," she said. "But we'll get in through this drain."

She held up a copy of a map. "We just follow this sewer pipe until we hit the number ⑦ line," she explained.

Trap stared at the map. "How did you get that?" he asked Pinky. I could tell he was impressed.

Pinky sniggered. "Goofsnout P. Goofus, my friend from school, made it for me. He is the assistant to New Mouse City's sewer control manager."

Suddenly, I realized what Pinky wanted us to do. "I absolutely **refuse** to go down into the sewers!" I squeaked.

GOOFSNOUT P. GOOFUS

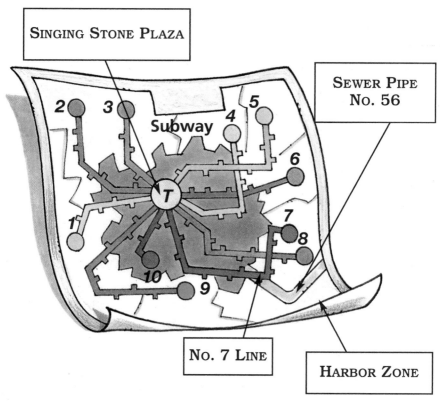

SINGING STONE PLAZA

SEWER PIPE No. 56

No. 7 LINE

HARBOR ZONE

Subway Map of New Mouse City

(T) SINGING STONE PLAZA

No. 1 line	Mona Mousa Street	No. 6 line	Cheese Avenue
No. 2 line	Fondue Arch	No. 7 line	First Cheese Square
No. 3 line	Paws-on-the-Nose Avenue	No. 8 line	Mouse of the Sea Avenue
No. 4 line	Daringmice Avenue	No. 9 line	Mackerel Street
No. 5 line	Chimneycaps Handwhiskers Street	No. 10 line	Saint Seed Pearl Street

"I am not a sewer rat! I am a respectable mouse!"

Trap rolled his eyes at me. "Well, I just call that **FEOr!**" he snorted.

"**F** as in WHAT A 'FRAIDY MOUSE!

E as in ENOUGH WITH THE DRAMA!

A as in ANOTHER SILLY EXCUSE
DOWN THE DRAIN!

R as in REALLY, GERMEISTER, DON'T
BE SUCH A WIMP!"

Then he added, "Just think about Sally. She may already be down there, stealing your *scoop!*"

Thea removed the grating and went in first. Pinky went next. I GROANED. I guess I had no choice. I had to go. I would never hear the end of it if Sally got the story. I followed Pinky's fading light. Trap insisted that he would go down last.

"I want to make sure that Mr. 'Fraidy Mouse here doesn't scamper off," he said. "It wouldn't surprise me. Even as a young mouselet, he was always *RUNNING* away from something."

I started to argue, but Thea stopped us. "Shhhhh!" she squeaked. "Shut your snouts and get going!"

CAT CAT
CAT CAT . . .

It was **dark** under the streets.

We climbed down an iron ladder one pawstep at a time. It was slippery. Very slippery. I was glad to be wearing those ugly rubber boots. So what if I was a fashion victim. At least I wouldn't break my tail.

The cold seeped through my fur. I sneezed.

"**Achoo!** *Achoo!* *Achoo!*

I knew it! I've already caught a cold!" I moaned.

Trap snickered. "Poor Gerrykins has caught a coldykins," he squeaked in a high-pitched voice.

I would have yelled back, but I was too **SCARED**. Did I mention I'm afraid of heights? Down, down, down we climbed. Would this tunnel never end?

"That's it!" Thea said at last.

I rested my paws on the ground. What a relief! If only I could head home now. Instead, I looked around.

We were on a very slippery, narrow

pavement. A canal full of smelly sewage flowed to our left.

Just then, Trap pointed to a spot behind me. "Geronimo! There's a **CAT** behind you!" he cried.

I shrieked in terror.

"Tricked you!" chuckled my cousin.

I chewed my whiskers, fuming.

Trap just snickered. "Lighten up, Gerry Berry," he advised. He began dancing around me in a circle. "Put your paws in the air like you just don't care! Kick up your feet and dance to the beat!" he sang.

I started to relax. Maybe Trap was right. Maybe I needed to stop worrying about everything. Maybe there really wasn't a phantom **CAT** in the subway. Maybe it was

A canal full of smelly sewage flowed to our left.

just a silly story. Yes, that was probably it. A silly story made up by some bored mouse with lots of time on his paws.

Just then, Trap leaned over and shrieked in my ear, "MEOW!"

MEOW MEOW MEOW MEOW MEOW MEOW MEOW MEOW MEOW MEOW MEOW MEOW MEOW MEOW MEOW MEOW MEOW MEOW MEOW MEOW MEOW MEOW MEOW MEOW MEOW MEOW MEOW MEOW MEOW MEOW

I nearly jumped right out of my wet suit! Why, oh, why was my cousin so *ANNOYING*?

CAT DOO-DOO

Thea was busy studying Pinky's map. "It looks like we have almost reached the end of this pipe. That means we should be crossing the number **7** line soon," she said. "Then we're off to Singing Stone Plaza, the beginning of the line."

We marched along slowly in the dark. Our flashlights made *GHOSTLY SHADOWS* on the walls.

Suddenly, I slipped on a dark spot.

"Got to watch out for that **CAT** doo-doo, Cousinkins," Trap joked.

I shuddered.

The liquid flowing in the canal gave off a horrible stench.

"It really smells like CAT doo-doo, doesn't it, Geronimo?" my cousin chuckled.

I ordered myself to stay calm. "Please do not say that word again," I begged.

Trap snickered. "What word, Gerrykins?" he giggled.

When I didn't answer, he screeched, "What's wrong, has the CAT got your tongue?"

I shuddered again.

"Come on, let the CAT out of the bag, Geronimoid!" my cousin shrieked. Then he stuck his snout up to mine. "Gee, you look beat, Gerrykins. Maybe you should take a little CATnap!"

Finally, I snapped.

"

Enoooooooooooooogh...

"

I squeaked at the top of my lungs.

My cousin looked shocked. You see, I am usually a pretty mild-mannered mouse. I don't like to make a big squeak about things. Still, even I have my limits. I mean, I'm a rodent, not a ROBOT. I have feelings, too.

I was sick of Trap teasing me. It was time for me to put my paw down. Yes, this was the moment of truth. The moment I had been waiting for since I was a young mouselet. I would finally put my cousin in his place. I cleared my throat. Then I gulped. Two enormous yellow eyes had appeared out of nowhere. They glowed in the inky blackness. They were staring right at us! **I let out a shriek of utter terror.**

"Heeeelp!!!

It's the

Phantom

Cat!!!"

I cried. I closed my eyes. When I opened them, the cat was gone.

How odd. Still, I heaved a sigh of relief.

Seconds later, Trap was up to his old *tricks*. Three times he pointed to a spot over my shoulder. "Geronimo, a **CAT!**" he cried. But he was only teasing.

We trudged on. Trap tried to *trick* me again, but I wasn't falling for it. When he yelled **CAT**, I brushed him off. But this time, he had a strange look on his face. My heart leaped to my throat. Slowly, I turned around. Behind me loomed the shadow of a monstrous **CAT!** Its claws shot out, reaching for us.

Was this it? Was this how my life would end? Was I about to become just another dead rodent clogging up the drain?

"Good-bye, mouse friends!" I sobbed.

*Behind me loomed the shadow
of a monstrous cat!*

LIKE A SEWER RAT

Just then, the shadow disappeared. No one moved. We were frozen with fear. Finally, we hid around a corner.

Thea gave us half an hour's rest to pull ourselves together.

Trap immediately began searching through his backpack. "This calls for some serious munching!" he squeaked.

Out of the bag came a cheddar pie, a bag of nachos, and a jar of mozzarella balls.

This was followed by **three large rolls**, a pineapple cheesecake, and a box of **MINT JELLY CANDIES**.

My cousin opened a thermos and chugged down the contents.

"Gotta love that pickled pepper tea!" he spluttered, smacking his lips.

He finished with some onion-flavored chewing gum. "It freshens the breath," he explained. Then he massaged his stomach and let out a loud **BURP!**

I know what you are thinking. How could such a *sophisticated*, civilized mouse like me be related to such an obnoxious, disgusting mouse? I have asked myself the same question many times. Unfortunately, I have not figured it out yet. Trap is definitely one of a kind.

I was still thinking about my annoying relative when Thea's voice broke into my thoughts.

"OK, this is it," she announced. "See that tunnel over there? That's where the number ⑦ line begins. But we'll have to cross the sewage canal to get there."

I stared at the canal. It was so dark. It was so smelly. "**I can't do it!**" I decided. "Sorry, Thea, but I just can't cross over that sewage."

My sister didn't blink an eye. In fact, she was already on her way. "Suit yourself," she said over her shoulder.

I ran after her. "Wait!" I shrieked. "You can't just leave me here all alone!"

Thea put her paws on her hips. "Well, then, come on, 'fraidy mouse!" she snorted. "I haven't got all day! Move your tail, or I'll tie it up in a knot!"

What could I do? I followed with my tail

It was so smelly!

between my paws. I was still scared, but at least I wasn't alone.

Thea threw a rope across the canal. The metal hook on the end of the rope grabbed the ladder on the opposite side of the sewer.

We crossed the canal, hanging from the rope. Luckily, it wasn't very deep. The STINKING liquid barely reached our snouts.

Still, the smell was enough to make any rodent lose his lunch. *UGH!* I was glad I had only eaten three cheese balls.

At last, we made it to the other side. We had reached the number 7 line.

THE CHAINS OF THE PHANTOM CAT

Just then, a terrifying MEOOOOOOWWWW!!! filled the tunnel. We heard chains clanking on the tracks.

The phantom **CAT** must be near!

My heart was tap dancing like Frankie Fastpaws onstage. **Why, oh, why** had I come along?

Suddenly, it was silent again.

At first, no one moved. We were all shaken. Then Trap began digging through his pack.

"A quick snack for courage," he explained.

He pulled some bread and a small tube. He squeezed a disgusting paste onto the bread. "EXTRA-STRENGTH GARLIC!" he explained with a grin.

We all leaped backward. The stench from that garlic was worse than the *SEWAGE!*

Extra-strength garlic!

KRUNCHIES! PULLEYS! JINGLE BELLS!

We headed toward Singing Stone Plaza Station. It was tough going. We walked in single file along a narrow ledge. It was dark and spooky. The only sound was water dripping creepily from above: PLINK, PLINK, PLINK!

"Stay clear of the rails," Thea warned us. "They are very dangerous. If you touch the third rail, you're toast!"

I shivered. My great-uncle Munchy had been struck by lightning in a rainstorm. His whiskers were completely fried off. Luckily, he hadn't lost his squeak.

We finally reached the subway station. The platform was lit by powerful floodlights. This is

where passengers waited for the trains.

Right then, we heard voices. We hid inside a telephone booth. It was a tight squeeze. I could barely breathe. If only my big-bellied cousin hadn't eaten such a huge lunch. I peeked out of the booth. It was Inspector Clue Rat and his assistant.

"We haven't found any pawprints, Inspector. Neither from a **CAT** nor a mouse," the assistant reported.

Clue Rat muttered to himself. His assistant rambled on.

He explained about the **CAT TRAP**. The feline psychology professor had come up with a plan. It

INSPECTOR CLUE RAT

involved four hundred boxes of **Kitty Krunchies**. "The Krunchies have been transferred to a **giant** box," the assistant said. "The box will be shaken by a system of pulleys. Then Inspector Darren Dimwhiskers, our colleague, will hide next to the box. He will ring a huge jingle bell to lure the **CAT**. Isn't that a great idea?"

Clue Rat looked like he was ready to explode. "**Krunchies!** Pulleys! Jingle bells!" he thundered. He twisted his tail up in a knot. "You call that a great idea?! You call that a scientific method?!" the inspector roared. "Well, I call that psychology professor a total **cheesebrain**!"

"Isn't that a great idea?"

But his assistant wasn't finished yet. "Well, we also have a loudspeaker that can broadcast 'Here, kitty kitty kitty . . .'"

The inspector just threw his paws in the air. Then he left in a huff.

I watched him leave. That's when I noticed what a mess the subway had become. The benches were crooked. The floor was stained. The walls were covered in GRAFFITI.

The subway system was built fifty years ago. Now it had fifty years' worth of *wear and tear*. I shook my head. This place needed more than just a few repairs. It needed a megamakeover!

"You call that a scientific method? A great idea?! You call that . . .

The inspector left in a huff.

SHOW YOUR SNOUT!

We were still in the phone booth when we heard more voices.

One was a female's. It was loud. It was abrasive. Yes, I knew that voice well. It belonged to Sally Ratmousen, my number-one enemy.

"I can't wait to beat *The Rodent's Gazette* to this *scoop,*" Sally snickered. "That nitwit Stilton won't know what hit him!"

I seethed with anger.

Sally was with her editor in chief, Pawsley Pinhead. The poor mouse was examining the ground through his magnifying glass.

"*Move your tail,* **PINHEAD**!" Sally shrieked.

Pawsley licked his whiskers. Sweat dripped down his fur. "Um, Boss, may I go and get a cheese ice cream from the vending machine?" he mumbled.

Sally thumped her tail. "Ice cream, my paw! START SEARCHING, PINHEAD! I want some clues and I want them **right now! At once! Immediately!**"

Just then, I felt a sneeze coming on. Quick as a flash, Trap held my snout with his paw.

Sally pricked up her ears. "I could swear I just heard Geronimo Stilton," she muttered.

May I get a cheese ice cream from the vending machine?

Cheese Ice cream

1. **Gorgonzola popsicle**

2. **Cheddar ice cream cone with a candied cherry on top**

3. **Fondue ice cream cake**

4. **Triple cheese ice cream cake**

"But, Boss, we're the only ones down here," Pawsley insisted.

Sally just pinched his ear. "Get to work, **PINHEAD**!" she squeaked.

Suddenly, we heard a terrifying meowing. It was the phantom cat!

Pawsley turned as pale as a piece of mozzarella. "I dare you to come out and show your ugly feline snout!" Sally shouted.

AS IF IN REPLY, THE LIGHTS WENT OFF.

So did Pawsley. He ran off in the dark. Sally ran after him. "Come back, you coward, or I'll fire you!" she squeaked.

"Get to work, Pinhead!"

ALL BECAUSE OF A BOOT

Seconds later, the lights flicked on again. We crawled out of our hiding place. Thea began snapping pictures. Pinky took notes.

All of a sudden, I spotted two **YELLOW** lights at the end of the tunnel. Was it the phantom feline again?

No, this time it was a subway train.

Just then, I heard someone **SHOUTING** for help. I looked down.

What was Trap doing down on the tracks? Had he spotted a half-eaten sandwich? I stretched out my paw to pull him out. Uh-oh.

This was no laughing matter. Trap's boot was **STUCK** in the metal grate!

"Slimy Swiss rolls!" shouted my cousin.

I lowered myself from the platform, trying to keep away from the rails. I had to get that boot off my cousin.

The train raced straight toward us.

"We're dead rats, Cousinkins," Trap sobbed. "So long, cruel world!"

Without a word, I began furiously undoing his boot.

There were twelve hooks . . .

One, two, three, four, five, six, seven, eight, nine, ten, eleven . . .

The train raced straight
toward us.

... twelve!

With a sharp tug, Trap yanked
his paw out of his boot.

We leaped back onto
the platform.

SaFe! And not
a second to spare!

CAT FOOD

Thea and Pinky came running toward us.

"Wow, BOSS, I was sure you were CAT food!" Pinky cried.

Ugh. There was that word again. *Why* did everyone like to torture me?

Thea held up her camera. "What a fur-raising escape, Geronimo! I've got it all on film!" she squeaked excitedly.

"This could get me the prize for the year's most spectacular picture! Ahem, which reminds me, I am glad you made it."

I SMILED. My sister likes to act cool, but I know she loves me deep down.

Trap walked toward me, limping on his

one boot. "Those were expensive boots, Germeister," he announced. "Couldn't you have yanked a little harder?" Then he punched me in the arm. Hard. I tried not to wince. After all, I knew it was his way of saying thanks.

He rubbed his belly. "That little experience made me hungry," he squeaked. "How about we get some **cheddar ice cream** to celebrate our survival?"

We headed toward the ice cream vending machine.

Meanwhile, Thea and Pinky were deep in conversation. "I wonder who was driving that train," Pinky said.

"I don't believe in GHOSTS," I heard Thea whisper.

"Me, neither," Pinky agreed.

A shiver ran up my tail. Was there really a

Two cheddar ice cream cones with cherries on top

ghost **HAUNTING** the subway? I must admit, I was pretty spooked out. Just the thought of it made me want to jump out of my fur! I am not a brave mouse. In fact, my sister, Thea, says I'm the biggest 'fraidy mouse she knows!

At the vending machine, I spotted something shiny on the floor. I picked it up. It was an antique silver ring shaped like a slice of cheese. Carved on the outside were the initials **P.V.**

It was an antique silver ring.

FOLLOW THOSE
PAWPRINTS

Right then, I noticed something else. A strange stain spread across the floor. No, it wasn't a stain. It was some kind of print.

"A pawprint!" Trap declared. "It looks the pawprint of a megahuge **CAT**!"

I felt faint. Not the "c" word again. No matter how hard I tried, I just couldn't seem to escape it. Maybe it was time for a pair of earplugs.

Thea snapped a picture of the pawprint.

"Look, there are more of them over there!" she squeaked.

We followed the prints to the entrance of the number ① line.

THE MYSTERIOUS DOOR

Was this the phantom feline's hiding place? I cringed. I wanted to run squeaking from the tunnel. But I didn't. I didn't want to leave without finding out the truth. Plus, I didn't want Thea to tie my tail up in knots.

The pawprints led us deep into the dark tunnel. Then, suddenly, they stopped.

"Look at this!" Pinky exclaimed. "The prints end right at this wall. If there really is a phantom **CAT**, he could have walked right through the wall!"

My fur broke out in a sweat. My whiskers trembled. It was all very strange. And very scary. Cheese niblets!

I needed a vacation. Somewhere sunny. And warm. And happy.

A terrifying sight snapped me out of my daydream. It was Pinky Pick. One minute she was doing tricks with her **YO-YO**, and the next minute she had disappeared. "**Heelllpppp!**" we heard her shriek.

We called her name. But she had vanished into thin air!

"There must be a secret passage somewhere," Thea decided.

She shone her flashlight onto the wall. She examined each stone. Then she pressed one.

Two seconds later, she had disappeared, too.

"I guess we're next, Gerry Berry," squeaked Trap.

I WAS PETRIFIED. But I didn't want Trap to call me a scaredy mouse.

Together, we pressed our paws on the wall. It moved!

ON THE OTHER SIDE WAS TOTAL DARKNESS.

"Is that you, Geronimo?" whispered my sister.

She switched on her flashlight. We were at the top of a long staircase. It smelled like moldy blue cheese muffins. **Pee-yu!** I hate stinky smells. Someone needed to use a mop and some Mr. Cleanrat in this place. Carefully, we made our way down the old steps.

At the bottom was a gigantic oak door. It had an enormous keyhole and a huge key in it.

Carved into the door were the initials **P.V.**

Thea pushed the door open with her paw. Then she took the key out of the keyhole. "I think we'd better take this with us," she declared. *"Here, do something useful for a change, Geronimo,"* she added, passing me the key.

I wanted to point out that I was already carrying half her stuff. I had all of her extra film, her big fur brush, and five different types of nail files in case she broke a pawnail. But I didn't say a word. I was too **SCARED** to argue. I hooked the key to my belt. Then I followed the others.

CONCENTRATED CAT PEE-PEE

On the other side of the door was a huge room. The architecture was magnificent. The ceiling was supported by huge columns. On each column sat a sculpture of a smiling mouse head. On the walls were paintings of scenes from the *Great Cat War*.

"How fabumouse!" I breathed, my snout turned upward. Then I tripped. Did I mention I can be a bit of a klutz at times?

Thea picked up the object I had fallen over. It was a jug labeled CONCENTRATED CAT PEE-PEE.

CONCENTRATED CAT PEE-PEE

"So this is where that stench came from!" my sister exclaimed. "I knew there was no phantom **CAT!**"

I noticed a row of jars and beakers lined up on a table. We were in some kind of laboratory.

One jar seemed to be glowing in the dark. "I bet that's some kind of **PHOSPHORESCENT** paint," Pinky remarked. "The phantom must use it to create special effects."

Just then, Trap found a switch on the wall. "I wonder what this does," he muttered. He switched it on. A deafening

MEOOOOOOWwww!!!

filled the room.

I jumped so high, I shook paws with the ceiling.

"Calm down, Germeister, it's just a recording," my cousin pointed out.

Thea showed us a wall of video recorders. "Look, this is how the phantom must keep an **eye** on everything. It's like his own personal security system," she remarked.

Meanwhile, Pinky had discovered a projector sitting on the floor. She switched it on. The shadow of a humongous **CAT** appeared on the wall in front of us.

This time, I didn't just shake paws with the ceiling, I kissed it! I couldn't help it. I knew the **Shadow** wasn't from a real **CAT**, but I was still scared. Trap rolled his eyes at me, but I didn't care. I had nothing to be ashamed of. After all, I am a mouse and I do not like **CATS!**

WHAT IS THIS
LEVER FOR?

We continued to look around the laboratory. It was filled with lots of strange mechanical devices. I was checking out something that looked like an old jukebox when disaster struck.

"What is this lever for?" Trap mumbled. Before you could say **"squeak!"** he had pushed it.

Suddenly, all the metal objects in the lab were drawn toward a huge magnet, including the big key that I had hooked to my belt! Soon I was stuck to the magnet like cream on cheese.

"Help!" I screamed. "Get me down!"

Quiet as a mouse, Pinky hit the lever again. Everything hit the floor, including me. I landed right on my head.

"Rancid rat hairs!" I moaned, rubbing my fur.

I was going to have a lump the size of Mount Cheddar.

Soon I was stuck to the magnet like cream on cheese.

Ah, It's a Long Story . . .

Right then, the door flew open. We all turned around in surprise.

An enormouse creature stood in the doorway. I gulped. No, it wasn't just any old creature. It was a CAT! A CAT who was twenty feet long and weighed five hundred pounds!

The head was huge, with pointed ears. The whiskers shook. The gold-speckled eyes looked cruel. In fact, they seemed to look right through us.

My heart hammered away under my FUR. My paws shook. I was about to faint in front of a monster-sized CAT!

I tried giving myself a quick pep talk.

Don't worry, Geronimo. It's not that bad, I told myself. *Maybe he's a vegetarian. Maybe he just wants to borrow a cup of sugar. Maybe he's lonely.* But I knew I was kidding myself. I mean, I'm not blind. I could tell this **CAT** meant business. Still, there was something different about him. What was it? Maybe it was his eyes. They seemed so fixed and glassy. Or maybe it was his fur. It looked so fake.

Just then, we heard a weird whirring sound. The cat marched toward us with stiff **ROBOTLIKE** movements.

Suddenly, he stood up on his hind paws. Then he grabbed his own hairy head and pulled it off!

Professor Paws von Volt

My mouth dropped open in shock. But I was even more shocked at what happened next. A mouse slid out of the **CAT**'s body and calmly headed toward us. Then he wrapped me in a giant hug. "*Geronimo Stilton*, my old friend," he gushed. "It's so good to see you again."

I could hardly believe my eyes. It was my dear friend Professor Paws von Volt! *Professor von Volt* was a brilliant scientist and inventor. We had met on one of my many adventures.

I introduced my sister, my cousin, and Pinky Pick to the professor. They shook paws.

"It's so nice to meet all of you," said the professor. "I feel like I already know you. You see, Geronimo is my favorite writer. I

THE PROFESSOR WITH ONE OF HIS INVENTIONS—AN EGG-COOKING MACHINE

EGG

love reading his tales of adventure. They're so funny, I *laugh* my tail off!"

I grinned. Professor von Volt is one of my biggest fans. I like to send him my latest books when they come out. But sometimes finding the professor is like trying to find a whisker in a haystack. That's because the professor is never in one place for too long. He is always moving his LABORATORY from one spot to the next. That way, no one can steal his secret discoveries.

"I didn't know you had moved your laboratory," I told the professor. I am usually the only one to know each new address.

The professor rubbed his head. "Oh, dear, I'm sorry, Geronimo," he apologized. "I've been so busy with my inventions, I completely forgot to call you."

"No problem," I said, smiling. I wasn't surprised. The professor can be totally absentminded. Once he tried to build a house underwater. It was sort of like a square submarine with a chimney. The professor was so busy working on the outside of the house that he didn't notice a shark had moved inside! Talk about a SCARY house guest!

The professor showed us some of his latest inventions. There was a super-powered automatic cheese grater, a paw massager, and a

steam whisker curler!

Steam whisker curler

"Can I try?" Thea asked, picking up the curler.

The machine let off a puff of steam.

"Wow!" Thea cried, checking out her perfectly curled whiskers. "I have to buy one of these!"

The professor chuckled. "This is only a sample," he explained. "When I get a patent for it, I will send you one."

As usual, the professor's inventions were all incredible. But why had he created a giant robot cat?

"Ah, it's a **Long** story," the professor explained. "Let me start at the beginning. . . .

MY LATEST
INVENTION IS . . .

"As a young mouselet, I loved to dig tunnels underground. I would dig tunnels to get to school. I would dig tunnels to get to my friends' mouse holes. I would dig tunnels to get to the cheese shop. When I grew up, my family sent me off to Ratford. It is the most *prestigious* university on Mouse Island. I studied **science, physics, chemistry, mathematics, history, medicine, and more**. After I graduated, I was still fascinated with tunnels. I came up with a plan. New Mouse City had so much traffic. Why couldn't we build a transportation system under the ground?

"The mayor loved my plan. They started

building right away. I helped. And that's when I made an important *discovery*. There is a network of secret rooms under the city, dating back to the *Great Cat War*. They were used for communication with the outside

when the town was under attack. I decided to make one of the rooms into a hidden lab. Here I can conduct my experiments on ELECTROMAGNETIC FIELDS. There are no electrical sources underground to interfere. It's the ideal location!"

I was impressed. Only a brilliant scientist like the professor would come up with such an amazing idea.

"Would you like to see my latest INVENTION?" the professor asked. We all nodded.

He picked up a small box that looked like a remote control. "I call this the Uoltinator. It allows me to move any object without even touching it," Professor von Volt said.

He pointed the device at Trap. As if by magic, Trap rose into the air.

"Look at me, I'm a bird! I'm a plane! I'm a flying mouse!" my cousin giggled.

Professor von Volt lowered him to the floor with great care.

"I bet you could make a lot of **DOUGH** with that thingy," squeaked Trap.

The professor nodded. Then he grew serious. "Last Sunday, someone discovered this lab," he said. "And that got me thinking. What if the **Voltinator** fell into the wrong paws? It could be a total disaster. Maybe the world is not ready for my invention yet."

The professor had decided to move his laboratory once again.

Voltinator

He had built the enormouse **robot CAT** to keep away intruders while he packed.

We all listened to the professor's tale. The only sound was my cousin munching on an onion and cheese sandwich.

At last, Pinky broke the silence. "So you were the one driving the subway train," she remarked. "And you projected those **CAT** shadows on the walls."

Professor von Volt held up his paw. "Guilty as charged," he admitted. "But today I am leaving. You won't have to worry about the phantom of the subway anymore."

At that moment, the door swung open. Sally Ratmousen and Pawsley Pinhead barged into the room. Sally took one look at me and **SHRIEKED**. "Stilton! What are you doing here?!" she cried.

CROSS MY PAWS!

Professor von Volt looked angry. "Well, well, Miss Ratmousen. Did you forget something?" he smirked. "After all, this isn't your first visit to my lab, is it?"

Sally turned pale. Then she put her paws on her hips. "Of course this is my first visit!" she squeaked. "I've never set eyes on this joint before. Cross My paWS!"

The professor shook his head. Then he switched on one of the machines.

"This video was recorded last Sunday," he said. "How do you explain this, Miss Ratmousen?"

The recording showed Sally and Pawsley rummaging through the lab.

""

Sally squeaked. "I've been **framed**!"

Professor von Volt sighed. "I didn't just fall off the cheese truck, Miss Ratmousen," he snorted. "You are a liar and a sneak. I can't have my experiments falling into the wrong paws."

He picked up a small suitcase and waved good-bye to us. I wondered where he would set up shop this time. In a grass hut? Under a lake? Somewhere in the Blue Cheese Mountains? You never knew with *Professor* von Volt.

Before he left, I gave him the silver ring I had found. Now I knew what those initials stood for. They stood for Paws von Volt.

"Thank you, Geronimo. This ring has been in our family for *generations*," my friend beamed.

At that moment, Sally raced over. "Listen Volt, I'll pay you anything for those inventions. Anything you want!" she shrieked. "Right now! At once! Immediately!"

When he didn't answer, Sally grabbed the professor by the tail. "You don't want this to get ugly, do you?" she hissed.

Again the professor didn't answer. Instead, he picked up the **Voltinator**. He used it to lift Sally into the air. *Then he set her down on a chandelier.*

Sally was fuming. *Uh-oh,* I gulped. She looked madder than my grandma Onewhisker when she found a mouse trap in her garden!

With a terrifying squeak, Sally leaped onto the professor. "Give it up, Volt!" she yelled, reaching for the Voltinator. "With this thing, I'm gonna get RICH, RICH RICH!

With a terrifying squeak, Sally leaped onto the professor.

And then I'm gonna rule the world!"

A picture flashed before my eyes. It was the front page of a newspaper. RATMOUSEN TO TAKE OVER THE WORLD! the headline screamed. RIGHT NOW! AT ONCE! IMMEDIATELY!

Just then, the professor threw something onto the center of the floor. A YELLOWISH FOG filled the room. It smelled like cheese.

"Don't worry," my friend called as he raced away. "It's just a Swiss cheese smoke bomb. It won't hurt you."

After a while, we found our way out of the laboratory.

Sally had a murderous look in her eyes. "You'd better watch your step, Volt!" she SCREAMED to the empty hallway. "I'm going to find you and steal all of your inventions one day!"

But I knew she wouldn't. The professor was probably halfway to the Mousehamas in an invisible boat by now. Yep, Professor Paws von Volt truly was one clever scientist.

A Scoop in the Making!

At last, the subway system was back to normal. Inspector Clue Rat closed the case. Rodents everywhere breathed a sigh of relief.

One month later, I received a package in the mail. It had a million stamps all over it. It must have come from very far away. Can you guess who it was from?

For Mr. Geronimo Stilton
Publisher, The Rodent's Gazette
17 Swiss Cheese Center
New Mouse City, Mouse Island
13131

Yes, it was from my dear friend Professor Paws von Volt. He had sent gifts.

There was:

- a steam whisker curler for Thea

- an interactive YO-YO for Pinky

- a pen with cheese-flavored ink for Trap. It was just perfect for a mouse like Trap. He always ends up eating his words!

And for me? Well, there was a tube with several papers inside. I ripped open the letter attached to the tube.

It read,

Dear Geronimo,
Please publish this letter of apology in your paper.
I would like to tell all of the residents of New Mouse City that I am sorry for scaring them. In addition, I would like to pass along these plans I have drawn to restore the subway system. It is my gift to the city.
Thank you again, Geronimo. You are a true gentlemouse.
Yours sincerely,
Paws von Volt

I smiled. Now, here was a *scoop worth squeaking about*.
I called my sister.

"Thea, we are still going to get our story," I announced. "Prepare the front page headlines!"

Special edition!!! Paws von Volt, the brilliant professor who designed New Mouse City's subway system, has presented the city with a renovation project! Turn to page 4 for all of the fabumouse details!

The special edition of *The Rodent's Gazette* sold like hot cakes.

I even received a call from Mouse Island's top movie company, *Fur on Film*. They wanted to make a movie about the phantom and Professor von Volt. They were offering a ton of money. Still, I didn't want to give away all of the professor's secrets. I turned down the offer. After all, I am a *gentlemouse*.

My cousin was beside himself. "How could you, Gerry Berry!" he squeaked. "We could be rich! We could quit this **RAT RACE**! We could be soaking up the **SUN** on the Swiss Cheese islands."

I just shook my head. I mean, some things are more important than money.

I Am a True Gentlemouse!

Six months went by. One day, I received another letter from the professor. It said,

Dear Geronimo,
I am about to leave on an exciting trip. I am doing an experiment on Time Travel.
Would you like to join me? You could keep a diary. Then you could write a book about our adventure.

The professor explained that we would go back to the time of the dinosaurs, and then . . .

Oh, but that's another story — and another book!

In his letter, the professor also gave me his new address. But it's a *secret*, of course. Yep, you can ask all you want, but I'm not squeaking! I promised the professor I wouldn't tell anyone. And, as I have already told you, *I am a true gentlemouse....*

ABOUT THE AUTHOR

Born in New Mouse City, Mouse Island, Geronimo Stilton is Rattus Emeritus of Mousomorphic Literature and of Neo-Ratonic Comparative Philosophy. For the past twenty years, he has been running *The Rodent's Gazette*, New Mouse City's most widely read daily newspaper.

Stilton was awarded the Ratitzer Prize for his scoop on *The Curse of the Cheese Pyramid*. He has also received the Andersen 2000 Prize for Personality of the Year. One of his bestsellers won the 2002 eBook Award for world's best ratlings' electronic book. His works have been published all over the globe.

In his spare time, Mr. Stilton collects antique cheese rinds and plays golf. But what he most enjoys is telling stories to his nephew Benjamin.

Don't miss any of my other fabumouse adventures!

#1 Lost Treasure of the Emerald Eye

#2 The Curse of the Cheese Pyramid

#3 Cat and Mouse in a Haunted House

#4 I'm Too Fond of My Fur!

#5 Four Mice Deep in the Jungle

#6 Paws Off, Cheddarface!

#7 Red Pizzas for a Blue Count

#8 Attack of the Bandit Cats

#9 A Fabumouse Vacation for Geronimo

#10 All Because of a Cup of Coffee

#11 It's Halloween, You 'Fraidy Mouse!

#12 Merry Christmas, Geronimo!

and coming soon

#14 The Temple of the Ruby of Fire

Don't miss any of my other fabumouse adventures!

Be sure to check out these very special editions!

THE KINGDOM OF FANTASY

THE QUEST FOR PARADISE:
THE RETURN TO THE KINGDOM OF FANTASY

And look for this new series about my friend Creepella von Cacklefur!

#1 THE THIRTEEN GHOSTS

#2 MEET ME IN HORRORWOOD

If you like my brother's books, you'll love mine!

**THEA STILTON
AND THE
DRAGON'S CODE**

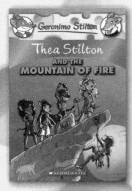

**THEA STILTON
AND THE
MOUNTAIN OF FIRE**

**THEA STILTON
AND THE GHOST OF
THE SHIPWRECK**

**THEA STILTON
AND THE
SECRET CITY**

**THEA STILTON
AND THE MYSTERY
IN PARIS**

**THEA STILTON
AND THE CHERRY
BLOSSOM ADVENTURE**

**THEA STILTON
AND THE
STAR CASTAWAYS**

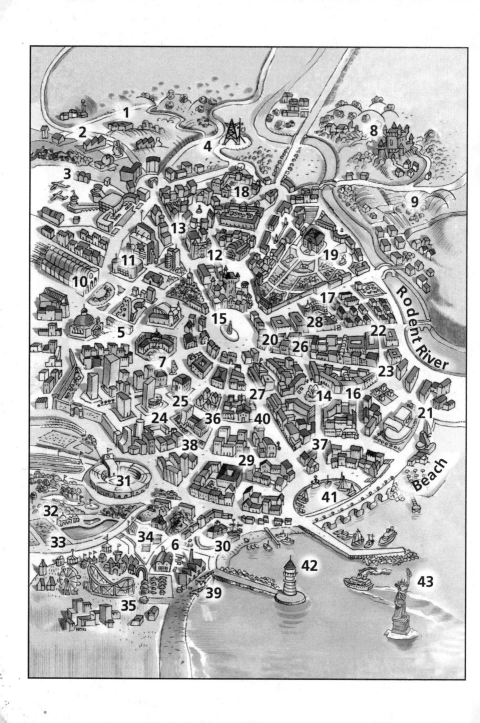

Map of New Mouse City

1. Industrial Zone
2. Cheese Factories
3. Angorat International Airport
4. WRAT Radio and Television Station
5. Cheese Market
6. Fish Market
7. Town Hall
8. Snotnose Castle
9. The Seven Hills of Mouse Island
10. Mouse Central Station
11. Trade Center
12. Movie Theater
13. Gym
14. Catnegie Hall
15. Singing Stone Plaza
16. The Gouda Theater
17. Grand Hotel
18. Mouse General Hospital
19. Botanical Gardens
20. Cheap Junk for Less (Trap's store)
21. Parking Lot
22. Mouseum of Modern Art
23. University and Library
24. *The Daily Rat*
25. *The Rodent's Gazette*
26. Trap's House
27. Fashion District
28. The Mouse House Restaurant
29. Environmental Protection Center
30. Harbor Office
31. Mousidon Square Garden
32. Golf Course
33. Swimming Pool
34. Blushing Meadow Tennis Courts
35. Curlyfur Island Amusement Park
36. Geronimo's House
37. New Mouse City Historic District
38. Public Library
39. Shipyard
40. Thea's House
41. New Mouse Harbor
42. Luna Lighthouse
43. The Statue of Liberty

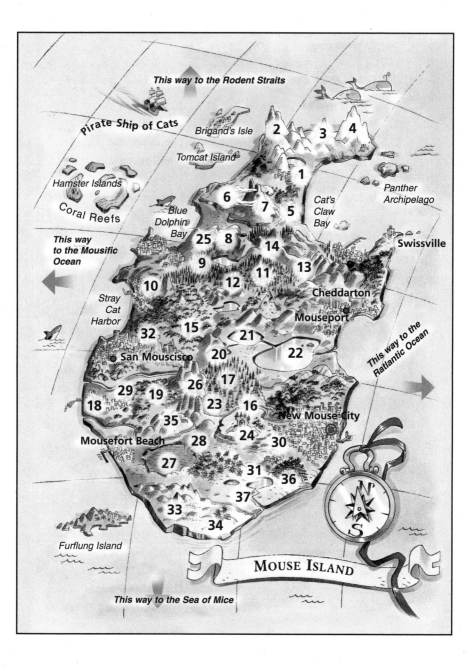

Map of Mouse Island

1. Big Ice Lake
2. Frozen Fur Peak
3. Slipperyslopes Glacier
4. Coldcreeps Peak
5. Ratzikistan
6. Transratania
7. Mount Vamp
8. Roastedrat Volcano
9. Brimstone Lake
10. Poopedcat Pass
11. Stinko Peak
12. Dark Forest
13. Vain Vampires Valley
14. Goose Bumps Gorge
15. The Shadow Line Pass
16. Penny Pincher Lodge
17. Nature Reserve Park
18. Las Ratayas Marinas
19. Fossil Forest
20. Lake Lake
21. Lake Lake Lake
22. Lake Lakelakelake
23. Cheddar Crag
24. Cannycat Castle
25. Valley of the Giant Sequoia
26. Cheddar Springs
27. Sulfurous Swamp
28. Old Reliable Geyser
29. Vole Vail
30. Ravingrat Ravine
31. Gnat Marshes
32. Munster Highlands
33. Mousehara Desert
34. Oasis of the Sweaty Camel
35. Cabbagehead Hill
36. Rattytrap Jungle
37. Rio Mosquito

Dear mouse friends,
Thanks for reading, and farewell
till the next book.
It'll be another whisker-licking-good
adventure, and that's a promise!

Geronimo Stilton